LIFE'S RAINBOW

"P.J." HORNBECK

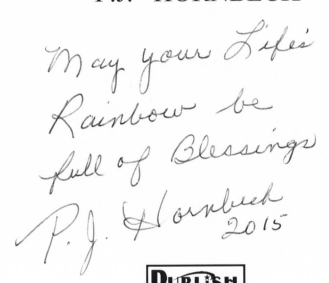

May your Life's
Rainbow be
full of Blessings
P. J. Hornbeck
2015

PublishAmerica
Baltimore

First printing

All characters in this book are fictitious, and any resemblance to real persons, living or dead, is coincidental.

ISBN: 1-4241-9833-X (softcover)
ISBN: 978-1-4489-8714-6 (hardcover)
PUBLISHED BY PUBLISHAMERICA, LLLP
www.publishamerica.com
Baltimore

Printed in the United States of America

DEDICATION

This book is dedicated to my beloved husband and best friend, who always encouraged me to write, and whose rainbow of life is over. May 6, 1938 - November 15, 2001

ACKNOWLEDGMENTS

All Scriptures and references to Scriptures have been taken from:

The New English Bible with the Apocrypha. Oxford University Press: Cambridge University Press, 1970.

The Holy Bible, New International Version. New York: International Bible Society, 1978.

FOREWORD

I have always loved to express myself in writing, although I had never taken it seriously. With the encouragement of my husband, I have put together some stories and events, including Bible verses and other writings.

It is hoped this little book is inspirational for all readers, young and old, whether you read it in part for a few minutes, or read it totally at one time. It is written with love for our Lord, Jesus Christ.

—"P. J."

PART I

THE BEGINNING

It was a typical winter day, extremely cold, with sleet, snow and a sharp northwest wind. The only heat in the tiny three-room, sparsely furnished upstairs apartment was that coming up through the registers from the apartment below. It was much too cold for what was about to happen.

The doctor yelled loudly, "How many times do I have to tell you to watch what you are doing and keep that ether mask over her nose and mouth? I'm trying to deliver a baby here!"

It wasn't uncommon to deliver babies at home during the Depression years, however, it was unusual to deliver them by cesarean section, especially when the only one to assist the doctor was the father of the child. The doctor was working feverishly to keep the mother alive. There wasn't time to call for an ambulance. It was up to him and the father to bring this baby into the world and try to save the mother.

Finally the baby was born; it was a girl. The doctor practically threw the baby on top of a nearby dresser. The baby was crying loudly and the father was concerned she would roll off onto the floor. He reached for her and the doctor screamed, "Don't worry about that kid, she will be OK; keep that ether going."

This was the start of my life's rainbow. I was named Patricia Jean. I don't know why, no one else in the family had that name. I guess my parents just liked it. The doctor was able to keep my mother alive, but because of the difficult birth and my father having to assist, I was an only child.

Being an only child is tough. You experience many hours of loneliness and are labeled as "a spoiled brat, who gets anything and everything you want." This is not true in all cases, certainly not in mine. I came from a poor family.

This was 1935 and the country was still trying to come out of the Depression years. There was one point in time when the only way the three of us survived was for my father to hunt and trap wild game to eat and to sell.

Finally he was able to get a job through the government, called the WPA program. Then things started to improve; however, my parents still struggled to make ends meet. Potatoes were cheap, so often we had fried potatoes for breakfast, boiled potatoes for lunch and fried potatoes again for supper. Daddy would go hunting when he wasn't working and then we would have a feast because he would come home with a rabbit or a squirrel.

Mother was a good cook. She'd fry up the game and make a water gravy, which consisted of grease drippings, flour and water. If we were lucky to have milk, she would fix milk gravy. What a treat! We had a bakery just a block from where we lived. On Sunday evenings Daddy would go there and see if they had any leftover donuts, which they usually had. They were rather hard and dried out, but mother would either steam them to soften them or make a bread pudding from them, which was delicious.

By the time I was six years old, I could see most of the kids in the neighborhood had some things that I didn't have, but the one thing I really wanted the most was a scooter, similar to those of today, only they did not have a motor. You pushed yourself along with your foot. Although some of the scooters were store-bought, the majority were homemade of wood, using two-by-fours and roller-skate wheels. My parents still couldn't afford to buy me one, but after much begging to my father, he finally consented to build one for me when he had time.

I knew Daddy worked long days of ten to twelve hours replacing railroad ties, so I doubted he would ever find the time to build me a scooter. However, one evening after supper I heard some sawing and the hammer pounding. I went outside to see what he was doing. I couldn't believe my eyes; he had started building me a scooter. I was so happy.

Now that I think about it, I was Daddy's girl, and yes, a little spoiled. If I'd ask for something, he'd try to get it or at least do something special for me. By the next Saturday my scooter was finished. I immediately took it out on the sidewalk and played all day long.

My mother called me in for supper, so I jumped off the scooter and went inside to eat. It was getting dark, and I was tired after playing all day. I took my bath and went right off to bed. I had disregarded previous instructions from my father: "Never leave your scooter out on the sidewalk when you are not using it. Always put it away in the storage shed." I left it outside all night long!

The next morning when I got up to go play, my scooter was gone. Someone had stolen it. I cried and cried. Daddy was loving and kind, but tough. This was definitely a lesson learned because he refused to build me another one. Needless to say, I cried myself to sleep for several nights. My scooter was gone! It really hurts when you have one of your treasurers stolen.

This certainly wasn't the only hard lesson he taught me. It was right after World War II and money was still hard to come by. So were jobs for my father. He also proved to me that I had to work hard to make my living in order to have those extra things in life that I may want.

I was given an allowance of 25 cents a week to dry the dishes and clean my room, as well as dust the furniture when mother did her weekly cleaning. One weekend there was a carnival in town and I wanted extra money to go. Daddy said, "You can work for me to earn it."

I replied, "Oh, yes, I'll do anything!"

My job was to pull grass from between a flagstone walk in our backyard. We had agreed that he would give me ten cents an hour. Within an hour's time I already had blisters forming on my hands. My hands hurt something awful and I had only made ten cents! I asked, "Is it this hard for you to make money?"

He said, "Yes, sometimes it is."

This was definitely another lesson learned. I pulled grass about another hour longer and finally made twenty cents.

World War Two (WWII) was over and the troops were coming home. There was once again a shortage of work for everyone, as well as homes for rent or sale. My folks had been renting but decided to purchase a rundown house and fix it up, provided a friend would loan them the money.

Daddy was a honest man and a hard worker. The friend loaned him the money needed, charging very little interest. The house didn't have a bathroom, and there must have been six to ten layers of wallpaper on the walls. We all worked together at night to fix it up, and lived in one room while doing so. It looked nice once we got finished; however, it was located in a bad part of town known as "frog town," and it was fairly close to the Missouri river.

I suppose even in those days there were "gangs," although they were called a bunch of bad kids. I would usually walk to school and on my way home four or five boys would push me and laugh at me. I'd cry and naturally that made their abuse worse. Nearly every day I'd come home from school crying.

Daddy got tired of this. One evening he took his pocket knife and whittled me a little club. He said, "When those boys start to pick on you, start swinging. If you happen to hit one, don't stop, just keep on swinging. Don't you start crying either. If you do, I'll give you a whipping when you get home."

The next day I went to school with my little wooden club. On the way home the same group of boys came up behind me, and one gave me a push and laughed. I turned around and started swinging my club. I don't know if I hit any of them, but they scattered and I walked on home as proud as could be.

After that day the group of boys never bothered me again. In fact, they would walk me home. They said they would be my protectors. I couldn't believe my ears. Those bad boys were now my bodyguards!

Although I didn't have any brothers or sisters to play with, I did have a little mixed breed dog named Sport. Poor little Sport had to endure hours in the summer heat, dressed up in a blanket and doll hat, while I tied old lace curtains around my waist and put on a song and dance routine for him. I know it was uncomfortable for him, but he was my buddy and he tolerated it. How I loved to sing and put on those shows, even if it was only for my dog.

For four years we continued to live in that house near the Missouri River. My best friend at that time was an old fisherman, Mr. Nobe. In the summer, every morning I would run down to his boat dock and fish shack so I could go across the river with him to check his nets. We went in his row boat, and I would dangle my hand in the water, singing at the top of my voice. He would smile and keep rowing. I didn't wear a life jacket; no one did in those days, nor was the water polluted as it is today.

When we got back to the fish shack with a good catch of carp, buffalo, catfish, and rock perch, people would be standing in line to buy the fresh fish. Mr. Nobe was an artist in cleaning the fish, especially the carp. He knew just how to fillet them so there wouldn't be too many little bones.

There was also a huge cinder pile beside the railroad tracks, and near the fish shack. I don't know why it was there, but most of the kids in the neighborhood played on it. Mother told me never to go there, it was too dangerous, but gosh everybody else did, so one day I couldn't resist, and I sneaked off to play on the cinder pile.

The kids were all climbing up the pile and running down. I did the same, but one time I tripped and fell, sliding down on my stomach and scratching my face and arm. Now what was I going to do? I wasn't supposed to be there, and how could I keep my mother from finding out?

I ran home, sneaked in the back door, hurriedly went into the bathroom and washed my face and arm. I looked in the medicine cabinet and saw some mercurochrome (which was similar to iodine). I put some on my scratches and thought that would cover them up. It did, but it covered them with orange streaks. I knew I'd get a spanking for sure, but I guess I looked so funny, that all Mother could do was laugh.

While living in the house near the river, there were floods, and we were flooded out three times in eighteen months. What a mess! There was mud a foot deep inside the house, and dead fish and snakes in the yard. We finally got the house cleaned, but it stilled smelled. Probably the dead fish still in the yard was the reason for the terrible smell.

The city said they would come and clean up all the yards in this condition, but weeks went by and no one showed up. The smell was getting worse every day. Daddy went to City Hall and talked to them on several occasions, but all he got were promises. Finally, he took a shovel and wheelbarrow, scooped up the dead fish and snakes, and dumped it all in the middle of the street. This really got the city's attention and they were there the next day. Normally a citation with a hefty fine would have been given for doing something like this, but not this time. The city knew they had failed in their duties and had left yards in an unhealthy condition.

After that we moved from the house near the river into another one on higher ground. This meant a different school for me and the need to make new friends. Perhaps I should say new acquaintances. As I said before, it is hard being an only child and being labeled a "spoiled brat" by people whom you think are your friends. I was lonely and had to do a lot of things by myself, however, it enabled me to be somewhat independent; something that would help me later in life. Even so, you still experience times of depression and wonder, what is my purpose?

Later, I discovered my purpose was to follow Jesus' teachings and the Commandments, many of which I broke along the way. My rainbow of life continued, but there were going to be some hard times ahead.

Exodus 20:3-17
"You shall have no other gods before me."

"You shall not make for yourself an idol in the form of anything in Heaven above or on the earth beneath or in the waters below. You shall not bow down to them or worship them, for I, the Lord your God, am a jealous God, punishing the children for the sin of the fathers to the third and fourth generation of those who hate me, but showing love to thousands who love me and keep my commandments."

"You shall not misuse the name of the Lord your God, for the Lord will not hold anyone guiltless who misuses his name."

"Remember the Sabbath day by keeping it holy. Six days you shall labor and do all your work, but the seventh day is a Sabbath to the Lord your God. On it you shall not do any work, neither you, nor your son or daughter, nor your manservant or maidservant, nor your animals, not the alien within your gates. For in six days the Lord made the heavens and the earth, the sea, and all that is in them, but he rested on the seventh day. Therefore the Lord blessed the Sabbath day and made it holy."

"Honor your father and your mother, so that you may live long in the land the Lord your God is giving you."

"You should not murder."

"You should not commit adultery."

"You shall not steal."

"You shall not give false testimony against your neighbor."

"You shall not covet your neighbor's house. You shall not covet your neighbor's wife, or his manservant or maidservant, his ox or donkey, or anything that belongs to your neighbor."

Matthew 22:36, 37

"Teacher, which is the greatest commandment in the law?"

Jesus replied, "Love the Lord your God with all your heart and with all your soul and with all your mind."

This is the first and greatest commandment. And the second is like it: "Love your neighbor as yourself." All the law and Prophets hang on these two commandments.

John 13:34, 35

"A new command I give you. Love one another. As I have loved you, so you must love one another. All men will know that you are my disciples if you love one another."

TALENTS

I have always loved to sing. My first public performance was at the Ritz Theatre in St. Charles, Missouri. Once a week they held a talent contest, with ten dollars being the prize. In 1940 ten dollars sounded like a fortune.

I was five years old and my mother entered me in the competition. On the night I was scheduled to sing, she dressed me up in my only Sunday dress, and gave me a little umbrella to carry over my shoulder. I wasn't nervous, but I suppose at that age kids don't really get nervous. I went strutting out on the stage singing, "The Flirty Girty Watchmaker at the Jewelry Store." I received a huge applause, but I didn't win the ten dollars.

As the years went by I continued to sing and always sang at various school events. When I was fifteen and in my second year of high school, I decided to study voice at a college which was 45 miles away from my home. My parents did not have the money to pay the tuition, so I got a job after school working as a file clerk in a doctor's office. Because I had to work to pay for these lessons, I only had the time to take one lesson a week. My father drove me to the college every Saturday, both winter and summer, for the next two years.

I did not earn a degree but did receive several college credits, some of which I applied to my required high school credits. By doing this I only had to attend high school for a couple of hours a day during my senior year. This gave me the opportunity to work more hours at the doctor's office.

In order to earn these college credits, I had to give a recital in the college's main auditorium. Usually all students who were also studying voice were there to critique the performance, as well as friends and relatives. The auditorium was full and I was really nervous, but I tried to remember everything I had been taught, and I thought I was doing pretty good. One of the hardest songs in my recital was "Oh Mio Babino Caro," sung in Italian. I needed a lot of breath control. Then I heard one student, sitting in the front row, loudly say, "She'll never make it." I was determined I would make it, and I did. I often wonder if God sent an angel to sing that portion for me.

At the end of my senior year in high school I was dating and going to the local dances on Saturday nights. On one particular night a friend of mine asked the band leader if I could come up on the bandstand and sing with them. He said, "Sure, have her come on up."

I had never sung with a dance band before, and this was a twelve-piece band with brass, strings and piano. I sang "You Always Hurt the One You Love," and it seemed to be so easy for me. He was impressed and asked if I would start singing with them. Of course I was thrilled and said, "Yes, I'd love to."

When I told my voice teacher, Mrs. Jameston, fondly referred to as Ms. Jamie, she was devastated. She said, "You will ruin your voice. You can be a lyric soprano, and you need to continue to study. I want you to go to New York to study and then to Europe. This honky tonk band will ruin your voice."

Although my teacher was like a second mother to me, I didn't want to sing opera, nor could I ever afford such extended study; especially in Europe, so I quit the lessons. I have never forgotten Ms. Jamie, and I never will. No doubt, she is now singing with the Heaven's angel choir.

Since I sang with a local band for money, I was considered professional, although in my own mind I was a long way from being professional. However, I decided to write a letter to the *Arthur Godfrey Show* in New York City, to see if I could get an audition. They responded by setting up a date for me to be there. What an experience! I was eighteen years old, I had just graduated from high school, and I was going to New York!

My mother went with me to New York. We really didn't have the money to go, but we couldn't pass up this opportunity. We went the cheapest way we could, traveling on what we called "the milk train." It took us three days and nights to get to New York since this train stopped at every station along the way. We slept in our coach seats and ate the lunch and snacks we had brought with us. One morning we decided to treat ourselves by eating in the dining car. However, when we saw the prices of the food, all we could afford was coffee and a small bowl of oatmeal, which tasted like paste.

This was a very uncomfortable trip for me, since the day before we left home, I had fallen down a flight of stairs and fractured my tail bone. I sat on a pillow most of the way. However, just thinking of my upcoming audition seemed to lessen the pain.

We finally arrived at Grand Central Station on a Tuesday morning. It was rush hour. We took a wild taxi ride to our hotel. We were amazed that the driver wouldn't help us with our luggage and then had the nerve to say, "Where's my tip, lady?"

Believe me, we weren't used to that sort of ride, much less someone wanting a tip for doing nothing; however, mother gave him a quarter and a dirty look. You can imagine the expression on his face! It is a wonder he didn't give her a few choice words and a gesture in return.

It was a beautiful day in New York, and the day before my audition, I was walking on cloud nine, vocalizing every chance I got. I had completely forgotten about the pain in my lower torso.

We had read in the paper that one of the big band leaders, Vance Lopez, had a noontime radio show at the Taft Hotel on Broadway. Often during his show, he would interview hopefuls wanting to get into show biz. Paul, a young fellow whom I had met at the hotel, and myself thought maybe, just maybe, we might get interviewed. Paul, who was nineteen years of age, had also come to New York to audition for the *Arthur Godfrey Show*.

Mother and I got up extra early that morning, and met Paul in the lobby. We walked to the Taft Hotel. It wasn't that far away, and needless to say, we didn't have the money for another wild taxi cab ride.

When we reached the hotel we stood in line for a couple of hours. There were a lot of hopefuls wanting a chance to be on Vance Lopez's radio show. Somehow we managed to get a table up front. Mother decided to take a table in the back of the room. She thought I might be embarrassed if she sat with Paul and me. She said, "I don't want Mr. Lopez to think you had to bring your mommy along as chaperone."

I was so excited and prayed Mr. Lopez would talk to us, which he did; however, it was not during the radio show. He no doubt had recognized the youthful eagerness in our faces, and the look of innocence. Then he sat down at our table. I couldn't believe I was actually going to talk to Vance Lopez! Little did I know that I was also going to learn some facts of life about being in show business.

Although Mr. Lopez was talking to both of us, he seemed to direct his comments mainly to me.

"Hello, I am guessing you came here to get on my radio show?" said Mr. Lopez.

"Oh, yes, if only we could!" Paul and I almost said this in unison. It was evident that we were both very excited, and nervous.

"I suppose you are both singers?" he asked.

"Yes, and we plan to audition for the *Arthur Godfrey Show*." Again we were almost in unison with our response.

Mr. Lopez said, "I'm sure you are both very good singers and ambitious, but let me take a few minutes to tell you just what you might be getting into. No doubt you have great talent, and are willing to work very hard. That is important; however, it may not be all that is required of you. To be a star you often have to travel a long, hard road. First of all, you will need to get an agent who can put you in contact with some people that can help to promote you, but let me tell you, some of these people may require favors from you. You are a very attractive young lady, and you a handsome young man, but being young and fresh, you may be asked to do certain things that would be against your morals. You could find yourself to be a piece of flesh that is bought and sold in the industry. You may find you no longer have control over your life. Show business is a world all its own, and often not a very nice one, and definitely not an easy one. Give it thought before you get too deeply involved. Stop and think just what you are willing to do to be a success."

With that he ordered us lunch, paid for it, and excused himself. Paul and I ate our lunch, then walked back to our hotel, not saying much, but thinking. Mother didn't ask us what happened. She could tell we were deep in thought.

I didn't have to think about it for very long. I knew right then that God had not given me a voice in order to lower myself to do the things that Mr. Lopez indicated might be required of me, and I would not compromise my beliefs and morals. Yet, I had come to New York to audition for a show, and that was what I was going to do.

That night I could hardly sleep. I kept thinking about the audition, the song I would sing, how I would stand, how I would hold my hands, and thinking I must remember to smile. Finally morning came.

The studio where I was to audition was just around the corner from my hotel, so I was able to walk there. This was good because I could do some deep breathing exercises on my way. When I arrived I was sent to a long corridor lined with folding chairs. There must have been twenty or more singers ahead of me and a long line behind me. I sat down and waited, making certain I sat very straight so my deep breathing could continue.

The girl sitting beside me was from Carolton, Florida. She was also eighteen years old. Her name was Della, and on weekends she had sung with a local band. Della had given up her regular job as a sales clerk, and it had taken all of her savings to come to New York, where she just knew she would become a star. We had been waiting for over an hour when Della was called into the auditioning studio. Within a couple of minutes she came out crying, and told me, "They didn't even let me finish my song!" I was next.

I was called into a huge room, or least it seemed huge to me at the time. In the middle of the room was a piano. Up above and to the right side was an enclosed glass area with three people, one woman and two men. They told me to give my music to the piano player and to face one of the walls, where there was a camera. I took a deep breath and nodded to the piano player that I was ready to begin.

I thought that a song from a Broadway hit would make a better impression than one of the pop songs I had been singing with the band or one of the opera arrangements in a foreign language. I chose to sing "Make Believe" by Jerome Kern. I was very pleased with myself and felt in my heart that I had done the best I could do.

The three people in the audition booth let me sing completely through my song and told me, "Thank you. When we find a spot on the show for you, we will give you a call."

I couldn't believe my ears. Had I passed my audition? Would I really be called to appear on the *Arthur Godfrey Show*? I wondered how long it would be before I received my call, and to what I thought may be stardom. All I could think of was receiving that call. I had forgotten what Vance Lopez had told me.

I never saw Paul anymore, and I don't know if he even went to his audition. He never appeared on the *Arthur Godfrey Show*, so if he did attend the audition, I suppose he didn't make it.

I waited for months, which turned into a year, but the call to come back and be on the show never came. Then I remembered what Mr. Lopez had told me, and I knew he was right. If I really wanted to move on into the entertainment world, I should have obtained an agent and aggressively pursued my chance to get on the *Arthur Godfrey Show*, as well as other shows. However, deep in my heart I guess I knew this really wasn't what I wanted to do.

I continued to sing another year with the dance band, and worked days at a local bank. To work by day and sing at night with only a few hours sleep was just too hard and it started to affect my health, so I quit singing with the band. I certainly didn't give up singing; after all, God gave me a talent and I was going to use it. I devoted my singing to the church choir, weddings, and local events.

Since that time several people have said, "Oh, I wish I had your talent." Talent is not just singing, playing an instrument or perhaps painting a picture. We all have talents that God has given us. It can be a talent of speaking, listening, being a friend, giving of ourselves, or being able to laugh and to cry.

Our whole life is a gift, and a talent given to us from God.

Romans 12:6-8

"We have different gifts, according to the grace given us. If a man's gift is prophesying, let him use it in proportion to his faith. If it is serving, let him serve; if it is teaching, let him teach; if it is encouraging, let him encourage; if it is contributing to the needs of others, let him give generously; if it is leadership, let him govern diligently; if it is showing mercy, let him do it cheerfully."

1 Corinthians 12:4-11

"There are different kinds of gifts but the same spirit. There are different kinds of service, but the same Lord. There are different kinds of working, but the same God works all of them in all men. Now to each one the manifestation of the Spirit is given for the common good. To one there is given through the Spirit the message of wisdom, to another the message of knowledge by means of the same Spirit, to another faith by the same Spirit, to another gifts of healing by that one Spirit, to another miraculous powers, to another prophecy, to another the ability to distinguish between spirits, to another the ability to speak in different kinds of tongues, and to still another the interpretation of tongues. All these are the work of one and the same Spirit, and he gives them to each one, just as he determines."

PART II

Jesus declared, "I tell you the truth, unless a man is born again, he cannot see the Kingdom of God" (John 3:3).

BORN AGAIN

"What have you been doing?" my mother demanded. "What have you and that boy been doing? Have you been fooling around?" With that she slapped me hard.

"No, no, I haven't done anything wrong," I cried.

"Well, we'll see about that. I'm taking you to a doctor, young lady."

It was 1948, and I was thirteen years old. In those years, it seemed that girls were allowed to start dating once they reached their teen years, and I had just started dating a boy three years older than myself. His name was Dale. We lived on a farm at the time and there wasn't much to do, except go to a nearby town for ice cream and ride around the town square in his little 1935 Ford Coupe. There wasn't even a movie nearby.

This was the first boy I had ever dated and immediately fell "in love." I suppose we both thought we were soul mates. We even discussed getting married. However, we knew because of our young age our parents would never give permission, so we thought we would elope after he graduated from high school. That was just one year away, so we talked and planned our lives together.

During this time my menstrual periods stopped. My mother was extremely upset, and after missing two of my menstrual periods, she suspected I was pregnant. However, how could this be? Dale and I had never done anymore than a lot of kissing. We never had intercourse. We were both too scared to do that. Besides, in my days of growing up, abstinence was the rule, and you were to wait until you got married to have sex. My mother and father were hard disciplinarians and I knew not to go against their rules.

The next week my mother took me to the doctor. When he examined me, I was so embarrassed. I had never been to a doctor for anything like this before, and the examination hurt so badly I was about to cry. The doctor then said to my mother, "The hymen is intact. I would judge that due to her young age the periods are just in the process of getting regulated. We can give her some medication and a shot every month to induce the periods on a regular cycle."

The medication and shots continued for six long years. I went to several other doctors during this time but none of them actually diagnosed the real problem. They would shrug it off and give me either a shot or medication to induce the periods.

In 1950 my parents sold the farm where we lived and purchased a grocery store in a town about 45 miles away. We moved there when I was in my second year of high school, and Dale had graduated. Our hearts were broken with this separation. Here I was, in a different town and a different school. I hated it!

Dale and I were determined not to be separated. Then my mother found some notes we had written with plans of our elopement. Needless to say, this did not happen. My parents quickly put a stop to it. I was wearing Dale's class ring and my parents made me mail that back to him with a note that I was no longer allowed to see him, and he was to no longer to have any contact with me.

I cried and cried, and I wouldn't eat and I wouldn't talk to them. This went on for nearly a week. Of course being a teenager in a grocery store with candy, cookies, soda and ice cream, I couldn't resist, and since I was getting hungry, I had to sample the goodies. This seemed to help ease the pain of not being able to see Dale anymore.

My parents tried to explain I would find new friends. They were right. It took me about two or three weeks, and once I got acquainted in the new school, I did find new friends and got involved in school activities.

This ended my romance with Dale, but I think I always held that young fellow close to my heart, but then doesn't everyone remember their very first love?

At the age of nineteen, I was still having infrequent menstrual periods. Then I noticed I was having trouble seeing out of my right eye. It felt like it had a cloudy film or a glaze over it. When I went for my next yearly eye exam, the doctor immediately saw there was something wrong, but not with the eye, and advised that I get to a medical doctor as soon as possible.

The next stop was to see my family medical doctor, who took x-rays of my head and then consulted with a neurosurgeon. Their finding was a brain tumor on the pituitary gland. The doctor estimated that this tumor had been growing since I was eleven or twelve years of age; thus the reason for the lack of menstrual periods and the loss of clear vision in my right eye. The tumor was pressing on the optic nerve. It had even enlarged the bone cavity at the base of the brain.

The year was now 1955, and in those days a brain tumor usually meant an operation, which often left the patient with some sort of disability, or even sudden death. My family certainly always believed in God, and we all went to church once in a while; however, neither my mother, father, nor myself had ever publicly professed our faith in Jesus Christ, our Lord. We never prayed openly, and the only prayer offered was the child's prayer that I would give before suppertime, "God is Great, God is Good, and we thank Thee for this food. Amen." As I got older, this too was omitted from our daily routine. Now though, we needed something to help us through this terrible ordeal that was facing us.

When I met with Dr. Roulak, my neurosurgeon, he proceeded to describe what would be involved with my forthcoming operation. I couldn't stand it. I cried and screamed, "I don't want my head cut on!"

I was hysterical. He tried to calm me and said, "It may not be any worse than a belly operation."

He didn't convince me. I didn't want to be operated on! Finally Dr. Roulak said there was a procedure whereby he could try to burn the tumor. This was known as x-ray therapy. X-ray therapy can be compared to radiation treatments of today and was sometimes used to a lesser extent after brain surgery.

Dr. Roulak said he would first try the x-ray therapy to see if the tumor could be reduced or completely burned away, although this had never been used exclusively without an operation. He went on to advise me that this was dangerous and my life was basically in the hands of the x-ray technician.

The dosage would periodically be increased and administered in three places, my forehead, the right side of my head and the left side of my head. If the technician set-up the procedure incorrectly, or if it was set it up to be administered at the back of the head, I could die instantly. I didn't care, I didn't want my head cut on. Dr. Roulak also warned me, if my vision got worse in the right eye, he could wait no longer and would have to operate immediately.

I started my x-ray therapy. My vision was checked every day and by the third day, it had worsened. In fact, I couldn't even see the big "E" on the eye chart. Dr. Roulak said, "We have to get the operating room ready now!".

"No, no, please, give it one more day. Please," I cried.

"Alright," he said. "We will wait one more day, but we cannot wait any longer than that. I will exam you first thing in the morning and if the vision is no better, I must operate. I am going ahead and schedule the operating room".

That night I slept very little, but I prayed and sought God's help. Never had I felt so close to the Lord. I know that my parents were doing the same thing, praying and asking God for his guidance and help.

The next day when my vision was checked, I could see the big "E" on the chart, and from that day forward the vision got increasingly better. God had indeed heard our prayers and answered them; proof that there is power in prayer. For my parents and me, this was a miracle!

My treatments continued for three months. Although I lost my hair on both sides of my head and had a huge brown burn spot on my forehead, I never felt sick and I did not have pain. However, once in a while I would feel a little lightheaded when I would bend over.

During this time, Dr. Roulak wanted to continue to observe my condition each day. He was able to get me a job in the St. Helen Hospital, where I had been a patient. I filed records, took care of the blood bank, and typed up lab reports. I earned $180 a month, and lunch was included.

I certainly needed a strong stomach to work there. Every day at approximately 11:00 a.m. the specimens from the operating room were brought into the lab. Although I may have been busy typing reports from a Dictaphone, every specimen went right by my desk. Then it was my lunch time! I'd go to the cafeteria and it seemed that every day they either had split pea soup or chopped suey for lunch. To this day, I can't eat either one.

Dr. Roulak and several other doctors continued to observe my condition for a little over three months. I also agreed to various other tests which could possibly benefit others who may have this same type of brain tumor. Later Dr. Roulak documented my case in one of the medical journals. Hopefully my experience enabled others to avoid going through serious brain surgery.

Once my treatments and observations had ended, I was able to come home, although I continued to be under Dr. Roulak's care for ten more years. He wanted me to come to him for check ups each year to insure the tumor did not return. If it had returned, he felt that more treatment could be given to burn it away once more. However, it did not return. Thanks be to the Lord.

My parents and myself went on to profess our faith in Jesus Christ and were baptized in the Presbyterian church. My father served as a deacon and an elder in the church, and I used my voice to sing praises to the Lord every Sunday.

Later in life I too became an elder in our local Presbyterian church, a member of the choir and was also given approval by the higher church to administer Holy Communion.

I heard a pastor once say, "You have to be lost to be born again." My parents and I were certainly lost, and reaching out to God for Help. So many people do not find God until they need that strength from the Holy Spirit. Strength is there; all you have to do is ask.

"O Lord my God, I called to you for help and you healed me" (Psalm 30:2).

SALVATION RENEWED

"I do not understand what I do. For what I want to do, I do not do, but what I hate, I do—As it is, it is no longer I myself who do it, but it is sin living in me" (Romans 7:15 and 7:17).

I suddenly found myself feeling like a piece of trash that needed to be recycled. It all started when I got married. I was twenty-one years old and he was twenty. From the first day Sam and I met he said he was going to marry me. At the time I didn't feel the same way; however, later on, after I started knowing and dating him, I thought I loved Sam, but I know now this was a false type of love. It seemed like all of my friends were getting married, and when Sam gave me a ring, I immediately said "Yes."

It was a beautiful and warm day in February when we married, but from the beginning it was not a sound or comfortable marriage. Even on our wedding day he kept saying, "If it doesn't work out, we will just get a divorce." I should have recognized then that the wedding vows were just words to him.

Sam was in the Navy on a four-year tour (referred to as a kiddy cruise). Immediately after the wedding we headed for the Great Lakes Naval Training Center, Illinois, where he was stationed.

We lived in a two-room upstairs apartment, over a very nice Polish family. Sam got a part-time job at a drive-in theater, or so he said. I got myself a job on base as a secretary in the legal department. I would come home, prepare a meal, and wait and wait. Finally I'd eat, then sit up a while longer waiting for Sam to come home. Often he would not show up until the wee hours of the morning.

When he did come home, I could tell he had been drinking. He would then wake me wanting sex, and would treat me like a whore, making me do sexual things I never dreamed I would do, nor did I know how to do. I never came from this type of background. It was disgusting. I'd often feel sick. Afterwards I'd cry myself to sleep. He would never say, "I'm Sorry," and I can never remember him saying, "I love you." I thought because I was his wife, it was my duty to keep him happy no matter what.

I continued to be left alone so much of the time, and never saw any of the extra money he should have been making. I started to suspect he was being unfaithful, and his drinking continued, but I guess I just didn't want to face it. I was feeling ashamed, thinking I wasn't a good wife. I finally realized he had been cheating on me within a month after we were married. I was told it was one of the girls at a bar where he went.

We seldom went anyplace together, not even to a movie. We did have one couple we were friendly with, Carol and Jim. However, Sam seemed to even use Carol to belittle me. He'd tell me she could cook so much better than me, dress better than me, and she was so attractive. This only made me feel more strongly that I wasn't a good wife and that is probably why he cheated. Consequently, I never confronted him about his affair with the girl at the bar.

When we had been married six months, he got orders to ship out for Europe. I remained a true wife. I went back home and stayed with my parents, and I wrote to him every day. I continued to take my wedding vows seriously. However, he didn't. Even when he was overseas, he would send pictures and there were always girls either in the background or snuggled beside him. How could he continue to hurt me like that? Yet, I kept telling myself that when he got home we would do OK and we could re-kindle our life together.

When Sam returned Stateside he was assigned to the naval shipyard in Charleston, South Carolina. I moved there so we could try to start our life again. In Charleston it was soon the same pattern, only this time he would often say he had "the watch" and had to stay on base many nights, all night long.

We seldom went anyplace together. I worked every day and spent the evenings at home alone. Once in a while he would take me to the "Acey/

Ducey" club, when a live band would be playing. This was only to make him feel important because he would get the band leader to let me sing. I would be up on the stage singing, while he was drinking and telling everyone that I was his wife.

It was summer and my parents drove nearly 1,200 miles to visit us for a week. I was employed at the base so I took off work for a week to be with them. We all understood that Sam could not get military leave for the week, but I did expect him to be home in the evenings. He was home only one night, then gave the excuse again that he "had the watch" for the remainder of the week, and was gone for the rest of the time my parents were there. I don't know if they suspected something or not, but if they did, they didn't say anything.

Yes, his infidelity had started again. Started again?? It never quit. For some reason Sam always had a knack of making me feel like anything he did wrong was my fault. All blame was put on me. I felt both shame and guilt, although I didn't know what I had done wrong. My pride still wouldn't let me give up the marriage. I kept thinking things would change, but I was only kidding myself.

Within a year he was discharged from the Navy. He had served his four required years. We decided to go back and settle in our hometown. This was a small community of 1,200, and of course everyone knew everyone else's business.

Sam had worked in a grocery store when he was in high school. He had even helped my parents in their grocery store on occasion. He was an excellent grocer man. There was a small, established grocery store for sale on the main street of town. We both thought, if only we had enough money to purchase it, we could start a new life.

My parents weren't rich people, but they had some savings, so they agreed to loan us some money so that we could purchase the store. The loan was all very legal, with our signing a promissory note to my father. This note included an interest charge of 2%. Payments were to be monthly. Where else could we have gotten a loan like this!!

I never saw Sam so happy and work so hard. I thought our marriage was finally on the right track. It wasn't on that track for long. Once again I discovered he was having an affair. This time with an older woman who worked in one of the local restaurants, and who by now had become pregnant. I think the whole town knew before I did. That's the way news travels in small towns…very fast.

This time I confronted him, and we got into a huge argument. I ended up getting a bruised arm and a black eye. I took the heel of my shoe and tried to strike back, but he was just too powerful for me. It only made him hit me hard again. Then he told me I was like a limp dish rag when we had sex. I tried to perform the sex acts he required of me, but I suppose I wasn't "professional" enough. As I think back I wonder if he would have hired me out if I was better in bed. This was the first time he had physically abused me, but it wouldn't be the last.

Business at the grocery store was beginning to drop off. Gossip was running wild about him and the other woman. Although I had a full-time job, I often had to take the day off to run the grocery store, with his excuse being that he was going to purchase groceries from a warehouse in one of the larger cities. However, when he returned he hadn't purchase a thing. He and his pregnant girlfriend were shacked up at some motel along the way, or perhaps he had a new girl by now, I don't know. It seems he would tire of his women pretty quickly.

Once again any money made at the grocery store was being spent by Sam, with no record as to where it was going. There was no money to restock shelves and customers were few.

I was holding down a good job with a land title company, but my salary was not enough to keep the store going and to make the loan payments to my parents. There was nothing left for them to do, so they called the promissory note. We had to have an auction sale of everything in the grocery store, as well as the sale of the building, to pay them. I'm sure this was the hardest thing my parents ever had to do.

My mother and father wanted me to leave Sam, but still I hung on; I guess because I continued to feel shame that I hadn't made the marriage work.

Naturally, having to sell everything at a public auction caused us both to be very embarrassed. We decided if we moved to a larger city, we could get away from some of the small-town gossip and the problem of the pregnant other woman.

We moved to a larger city where we didn't think people would know us, but running didn't help. Sam still could not seem to stay at home. His pregnant girlfriend also moved to the same area, so he'd go see her at least once a week, and in addition had yet another girlfriend. I have a feeling he was beginning to tire of the older woman, who by now was very big from the pregnancy.

I have to give Sam credit, he was a worker and quickly got a job at one of the big grocery chain supermarkets. He easily worked his way up the ladder to a department manager. His boss at the grocery store thought we were the perfect couple, as did others. I have always been able to socialize well with people and could be a good hostess when called upon. In fact, his boss and his wife thought a lot of both of us and would have us at their home often for dinner and drinks.

This did not pacify Sam. He wanted more, so in addition to his job at the store, he started tending bar at a little neighborhood establishment on the south side of town, near an Italian settlement, called "The Knoll."

There was no doubt in my mind that his infidelity was continuing. Once again he was gone many nights, all night long, and as before, I never saw any of the extra money that he was making.

I was working as a clerk typist, using all of my small salary to make car payments, pay the rent, and buy food and clothing. It was nearly Christmas and nice gifts were always exchanged between my mother, father, grandmother, aunts, uncles, and cousins. Where was I going to get the money for these gifts? Stealing items and changing price tags were really a temptation for me, and a couple of times I gave into that temptation. I knew I had broken one of God's Commandants, but I just couldn't let my family know what was going on. This way I was able to get something nice for everyone…and no one knew, only God.

One Wednesday night I felt especially lonely, and since Sam was seldom at home, I decided to go to the bar where he was working. I caught a ride with a girlfriend of mine, thinking I could ride home with Sam when he got off work. When I walked into the bar, he said, "What are you doing here? Get out of here and go home!" He was furious with me.

I said, "How will I get home? I caught a ride with Kathy and she is already gone."

He yelled, "Get home anyway you can."

What I should have done was get in our car, that he had driven, and leave him stranded, but I didn't. I started crying. I suppose that softened his heart a bit and he called me a taxi cab. I got into the cab for the long ride home. I barely had enough money to pay the driver. That night, or I should say in the wee hours of the morning, he came home. He told me never to come there again during the week, and hit me hard, resulting in another black eye.

Of course I had very little sleep that night and I was to be interviewed the next morning for a promotion in my job. Needless to say, due to a swollen face from crying and an eye that was turning black, I didn't do well at the interview and didn't get the job.

Although the bar appeared to be off limits to me during the week, I was more than welcome on weekends. The owner and his wife seemed to really like me. They liked to hear me sing and I would lead the group (of course mostly drunks) in singing, and we would dance, sing and drink some more. On Sundays we would go to various houses for more drinks, food and merriment.

Did we go to church or even think of God? No way! I was slipping farther and farther away from my Christian life.

For quite a while I had suspected that the neighborhood bar owner and family might have been connected with the mafia. On one occasion, the daytime bartender was severely beaten, resulting in a broken arm, leg, and internal injuries. The next week the owner's nephew was arrested for operating a bookie establishment.

One beautiful spring Sunday we were invited to Lou's home. Lou was the brother of the owner of the bar. It was a lovely place in the country. We rode horses, drank of course, sang Italian songs, and ate.

Lou's wife, Ann, was so sweet, yet she didn't seem to fit in with the group. I really liked her. I went into the kitchen and helped her get some of the food prepared, and we talked. However, her eyes appeared to be so sad. I did manage to make her laugh once when I told her I couldn't get the horse I was riding to leave the barn, and no matter how much I would say, "Giddy up," he would just stand there. She seemed to enjoy me being there with her, having idle chitchat.

The following Wednesday I heard the news. Ann was found dead from a gunshot wound. Cause of death, an apparent suicide. I have always wondered if it really was suicide. Although she seemed sad, she did not seem the type to take her own life.

I suddenly thought, *I can't go on like this any longer. I've got to get away from this kind of life.* The next day I called an attorney and filed for divorce. Sam moved out, but only for two weeks. I didn't think to have the locks changed, and one day in the early morning hours, he moved back in, begging me to take him back.

I did not give in. Since I couldn't convince him to leave, the next day I found myself a little apartment and prepared to move out. After nine years of living like this, I could not take it any longer. The only things I took with me were my clothes and what I could put in the trunk of my car. I had an old upright piano that a great aunt had given me. I just couldn't leave it because of the sentimental value, so I got a piano mover to take it to my new apartment, which was in a very bad neighborhood, but that was all I could afford.

I suppose I got the worse beating from Sam the night before I moved. In fact, I thought for a while he might kill me. First he went to the closet and got his rifle, then he torn my dress off and pined me up against the wall, repeatedly hitting me. He then threw me on the bed and raped me, after which time he started yelling, "You aren't going to leave me!!" But I did.

People often ask, "Why did you continue to put up with that? Why didn't you call the police? Why didn't you put a restraining order against him? Why did you stay with him for nine years?

It is hard to explain "why." The only explanation is, you feel ashamed and embarrassed. You feel you have been a failure, and you just don't want to admit it.

Once I got settled in my little furnished apartment, I started back to church and began singing with the choir. I felt a burden had been lifted from my shoulders, and a feeling of peace came over me. My salvation had been renewed.

James 1:21
"Away then with all that is sordid, and the malice that hurries to excess, and quietly accept the message planted in your hearts, which can bring you salvation."

Romans 12:2
"Do not be conformed to this world, but be transformed by the renewing of your mind."

Psalm 40:1-3
"I waited patiently for the Lord, he turned to me and heard my cry. He lifted me out of the slimy pit, out of the mud and mire, he set my feet on a rock and gave me a firm place to stand. He put a new song in my mouth, a hymn of praise to our God. Many will see and fear and put their trust in the Lord."

I later heard that Sam had died a painful death of throat cancer, at an early age of 54. When I heard this I didn't cry, or even feel sad, yet I couldn't get him off of my mind. It seemed that all I could think of were our bad times together. I could not remember any good times. It finally occurred to me that I had never forgiven him for the hurt he had caused me.

I started praying to God. "Let me forgive him." Suddenly I no longer felt remorse or anger, but I felt sorry for him. I again prayed, this time that God would forgive me. After that I no longer thought of Sam. That part of my life was put behind me, as though it were just a dream.

Through God we can forgive, we can be forgiven, and our salvation can be renewed.

Matthew 6:14-15
"For if you forgive others the wrongs they have done, your heavenly Father will also forgive you; but if you do not forgive others, then the wrongs you have done will not be forgiven by your Father."

Ephesians 4:32
"Be kind and compassionate to one another, forgiving each other, just as in Christ, God forgave you."

PART III

LOVE

"I may speak in tongues of men or of angels, but if I am without love, I am a sounding gong or a clanging cymbal. I may have the gift of prophecy, and know every hidden truth; I may have faith strong enough to move mountains; but if I have no love, I am nothing. I may dole out all I possess, or even give my body to be burnt, but if I have no love, I am none the better. Love is patient; love is kind and envies no one. Love is never boastful, nor conceited, nor rude. never selfish, not quick to take offence. Love keeps no score of wrongs, does not gloat over the other men's sins, but delights in the truth. There is nothing love cannot face, there is no limit to its faith, its hope, and its endurance" (I Corinthians 13:1-7).

"In a word, there are three things that last forever, faith, hope, and love; but the greatest of them all is love" (I Corinthians 13:13).

"There are three sights which warm my heart and are beautiful in the eyes of the Lord and of men; concord among brothers, friendship among neighbors, and a man and wife who are inseparable" (Ecclesiasticus 25:1, from The Aprocrypha).

I believe it must have been love at first sight that beautiful spring day when we met. I was a secretary for the automation department, and this was his first day on the job as an electric accounting machine operator (EAM). I went to the main door to walk him up to his work site. Glen was at the front entry to the building, patiently waiting. What a handsome man, tall, dark hair, beautiful brown eyes, but oh so very skinny. I thought, *I'd like to fatten this poor guy up.*

I said, "Hi, I'm Patricia, but most people call me 'P.J.'"

He said, "I think I will just call you 'P'."

That was sort of weird because that is what my mother often called me.

From the very beginning we were comfortable when we were together, and became good friends. It seemed like every day we would talk and confide in each other. He told me about his life and his terrible childhood, which is something you only read about in books or in the newspapers.

Glen was the fifth child of fourteen children, and was born in southeastern Missouri. His father was an alcoholic. Yet somehow his father managed to hold a decent job at a flour mill, probably because the owner felt sorry for all of his little children, knowing they needed food and clothing.

Glen's father gave his mother $20 a week to pay the bills and feed and clothe the children. Needless to say, food and clothes were scarce. The kids didn't get shoes to wear until November when the cold days began. They were often hungry. For a school lunch Glen would have cold fried potatoes on a cold biscuit. He was so embarrassed when he saw other children with a nice lunch of a meat sandwich and fruit that he would often throw his lunch away, and go hungry rather than be laughed at by the other kids.

His father was abusive, and he would tell Glen he wasn't as good as other people. He would accuse Glen's mother of being unfaithful and yell at her that some of the children weren't his, that she was cheating on him. One time he even threw hot water on her. The kids could never understand why she would continue to stay with him. She was such a sweet and loving woman, and a wonderful mother to them. However, she wouldn't leave her husband. She always said, "No matter what, I love him."

The houses they lived in were rat infested. Rats would crawl over the beds at night. Glen's mother would tie blankets and rags over the top of the baby's bed to help keep the rats from getting to it. Two of the girls were bitten by the rats; one girl was bitten in the nose.

As soon as Glen was seven or eight years old, he had to start working in the cotton fields, chopping cotton and picking cotton. He was a small child in stature but a good worker, and often would have so much cotton in his sack that he couldn't pull it. His mother, who not only had the children and home to care for, also worked in the fields, and she would help him pull his sack of cotton up to the wagon.

Did Glen get to keep the money he made? Never! It all went to the father who would use it to drink and to feel important by furnishing drinks for his so-called friends at the tavern.

One summer, when Glen was seventeen, he was picking watermelons. He did such a good job that the boss gave him an extra dollar. Glen figured that dollar was his to keep, so he didn't give it to his dad, and certainly did not tell him about it. The next day Glen's boss saw his dad and said, "You have a good, hard working boy there. He picked so many melons yesterday that I gave him an extra dollar."

When Glen's dad got home, drunk as usual, he demanded the extra dollar that Glen earned. It was just too much! Glen decided he wasn't going to take this anymore. Although he had one more year of high school, he didn't go back. It was time he stared a better life for himself and asked his mother if she would sign for him to enlist into the Navy for four years.

Since he was just seventeen years old, it was a requirement to obtain a parent's permission. Luckily the signature of only one parent was required. His father never would have signed for him. After all, Glen was a good worker and brought in money for his dad's drinking.

Once in the Navy, Glen thought he had died and gone to Heaven. Although everyone else would complain about the food and conditions, Glen thought it was wonderful! He now had new and warm clothing and plenty to eat.

His older brother, John, had also gone into the Navy previously and was aboard the *USS Pickaway*, based on the West coast. God surely was watching out for Glen because he was also assigned to the *Pickaway* as a radarman. The *USS Pickaway* was a transport ship, making many trips to the Far East. Glen spent nearly his entire four years aboard this ship.

After his four year tour, he considered reenlisting, but he had a girlfriend who lived in southeast Missouri and she wanted him to come back home and get married. They did marry soon after he got home. She didn't want to stay in southeast Missouri; she wanted to go to the West coast and live. She had never been there; in fact, she had hardly ever been out of the southeast Missouri area. They moved to California, close to where Glen had been stationed. This move didn't satisfy his wife either. She didn't know anyone there, and she couldn't make friends easily. After a little over a year she

45

wanted to move back to southeast Missouri and be with her mother and people she knew.

Once they moved back to Missouri, Glen worked at the local flour mill, as did his father and almost all unskilled laborers in the area. Glen knew he could do much better than working with flour for the rest of his life, so he talked his wife into moving to St. Louis, Missouri, where he immediately got a job with the Federal government working in the automated data processing area. (This is where we first met and became friends).

Glen and his wife were married for four or five years, but it was never a happy marriage. She was a jealous person, not necessarily of Glen, but of what other people had. She spent an excessive amount of money on long distant telephone calls to her mother and friends in southeast Missouri, and often going back for visits without Glen. They lived from payday to payday, and beyond.

Then she got pregnant. The bills continued to stack up, especially the telephone bill. Glen couldn't figure out why she would need to make so many calls to southeast Missouri, supposedly to her mother. He nearly lost his job due to not being able to keep up with the payment of the bills. There were threats to garnishee his wages, but since he worked for the Federal government this wasn't allowed. However, he could have been fired because of it. Glen was a good and faithful employee and very well liked by his boss and all the people he worked with. Somehow he was able to hang on.

The baby came, and Glen was thrilled. It was a healthy boy. He went to the hospital the next day to see his bouncing baby boy, and both the baby and the mother were gone. His wife had arranged for an ambulance, and she and the baby had been taken back down to southeast Missouri to her mother's home, not letting him know.

They divorced and she remarried soon thereafter. This put doubt in Glen's mind. Was that really his baby? What about all of those telephone calls and visits to southeast Missouri? Were they really to her mother?

He never requested a blood test be run to confirm whether or not the baby was his. Child support was not requested in the divorce degree; however, he tried to pay a little each month. He found he just couldn't keep up with that. There were still a lot of bills that had to be paid: doctors, hospital, ambulance, and of course still many dollars owed on the telephone bill. He never knew for sure if the baby was his or not, and he never saw the baby again.

When he told these stories my heart ached, especially the stories of his childhood. I don't think I realized we were actually falling in love until I went on a two-week vacation with my parents. I couldn't wait to get back to see Glen, and he couldn't wait for me to get back. We missed each other so much it hurt.

He still had a lot of bills from his previous marriage, and we both had car payments, but we knew we wanted to spend the rest of our lives together. We were married March 19, 1966. It was just a small wedding in the local Presbyterian church. We only had another couple there as our witnesses. Afterwards, we all went out for a nice dinner. There was no honeymoon. We couldn't afford it.

As I think back, Glen must have loved me because when we got married I didn't have any front teeth. A few weeks prior to the wedding, I fell and broke out my two front teeth. Was I ever a sight! When I told my family dentist I was getting married and needed teeth right away, he laughed and fixed me up with a couple of plastic teeth to use during the wedding.

This wasn't the only time my face looked awful. Several years later, over one weekend, I lost the vision in my right eye due to a virus that had torn apart the retina. I was operated on, and for fourteen days, both day and night, I had to keep my head bent down. At night I slept with my head in a restraint-type contraption at the foot of the bed. In the morning when I got up I looked like something from outer space. My lips and the skin on my face was all swollen and hanging down. Although I looked awful, Glen never laughed. He was so tender and caring. We both prayed that my sight would return, but it didn't. I often say, "Maybe that is why God gave me two eyes, in case I lost one."

Like any married couple Glen and I had our ups and downs, but nothing serious. At the end of the day we never failed to kiss each other good night and give each other a hug and a love pat. We were always friends and as much in love as ever. We were inseparable; where you would see one, you would see the other. We shared everything, our love, our faith and our hobby.

THE HOBBY

"I can do everything through Him who gives me strength" (Philippians 4:13).

No doubt in this modern age of travel nearly everyone has flown, but not everyone has flown in an airplane they built.

Our hobby was building experimental airplanes. We built four over a span of 25 years. My husband, Glen, was a very intelligent and self-educated man. He didn't finish high school, but could read a book or instructions and understand and retain it. Not me. I could read something and forget it by the next day; however, I was a good "go for" and helper, as long as I was told what to do.

Glen acquired his pilot's license in the early '70s and flight tested every airplane we built. All of the airplanes were built in the garage, in the basement, in the family room, in the living room, in the kitchen. What I mean, there were parts all over the house. There may have even been some parts in the bathroom!

The fuselage of our first airplane was near completion and sitting in our garage. The wings were in our basement, so we brought them out to the garage and bolted them onto the fuselage. After all, we had been working on this for nearly four years and we wanted to see how it looked. The width of the plane, with the wings on, far exceeded the two-car garage door. However, the entire plane did fit inside the garage, with six inches on either side of the wing tips.

We opened the garage door to take a picture of our accomplishment. Our nosey neighbor who lived across the street must have been watching every move we made because when she saw that plane in the garage, with wings on it, she couldn't believe it. She immediately called the news media and told them we had built an airplane in our garage and couldn't get it out!

Soon the news truck was in front of our home and they were unloading cameras, thinking they would get a comical story. However, they didn't. We proved to them the wings were detachable and the fuselage could easily be moved from the garage onto a trailer and taken to an airport for final construction. They still seemed to be interested that we had actually built this bird, but we didn't make the evening edition of the paper, nor the TV news that time.

The first home-built airplane was a Vari Eze, designed by one of the greatest designers of our day, Bert Rutan. This was in the 1970s. The Vari Eze was a foam and fiberglass airplane. At that time we had to build everything from scratch, cut out or hot wire the foam pieces, and lay up all fiberglass cloth with epoxy. It took us four years to build that plane, but it was worth it.

What joy we got out of flying that little two place bird. The Vari Eze looked like something from outer space. People would flock around it when we would land at various airports. On one occasion traffic on the highway stopped to watch that strange thing flying.

I can remember two scary times when flying the Eze. It was near the end of winter and signs of spring were starting to appear. A group of us had flown to Alton, Illinois, for breakfast. This wasn't far, but it meant flying across the river where the Missouri and Mississippi waters met. While in Alton, there was a freakish snow storm.

We were stranded at the airport until about 2:00 in the afternoon. We were then given only ten minutes to get airborne. Once in the air it was still very difficult to see, especially when crossing the river. Visibility was only a few feet ahead and the canopy was frosting up. Finally we got across the river and landed at our based airport. We then discovered there was some ice on the wings. We couldn't believe we had made it across the river with this ice. Surely an angel was flying with us that day.

The other experience was on an extremely hot day. We had flown to the Boot Heel of Missouri, almost to Tennessee, for lunch. On the way back home we decided to stop at Cape Girardeau, Missouri, to visit some relatives there. Once we landed and tried to open the canopy, it wouldn't open.

Because of the extreme heat, the plexiglas had expanded and seemed to completely seal the canopy.

The temperature inside was getting hotter and hotter to the point that we could hardly stand it. We thought if we both kicked the canopy together that we might be able to get it open, although we knew we would also break it. First we tried one more time to open it. We heard a little pop, and it opened. We both took a deep breath and said, "Thank you, Lord."

After ten years of flying the Eze, we donated it to the St. Louis Aviation Museum. It was displayed at various times in the Union Station, St. Louis, Missouri, as well as the St. Louis Art Museum, and several other places around the St. Louis and surrounding areas. The St. Louis Aviation Museum still has it, but it doesn't look very good anymore.

In the year of the big flood there, I believe it was 1993, wings of the Eze were swept away and the fuselage damaged. After the water receded, one wing was found right away, but the other one wasn't found until a couple of years later. A farmer found it up river in one of his fields. I understand the Eze was never repaired back to its original state, but the display tells of the flooding and what happened to it.

Our second airplane was a Glasair with retractable gear. This was a fast flying machine, cruising at approximately 200 miles per hour. This aircraft was again foam and fiberglass construction and took us only three years to build. Of course by now we had some experience in building airplanes and the hobby had really gotten into our blood.

We both decided it would be a good idea if I took some flying lessons just in case I had to land the plane someday. I had a young and an excellent instructor. He knew I was used to flying and already knew how to fly straight and level and make some turns. I also knew how to use the radio and could call in my position to the tower and receive instructions. My husband had taught me that much; however, it is never wise to have your husband try to teach you to land an airplane, or maybe even drive a car. It seems they always think you should know more than you do at the time, and of course you never do it quite the way they think you should.

I took twelve hours of flight training until I was able to take off and land without damaging the airplane. I even took a few lessons from the right seat because I knew if I ever had to land the plane, that is where I would be sitting.

I didn't continue on to get my license because all I thought I wanted to do was to be able to land. However, today, I wish I had my license. Some people say it's not too late to get my license, but it is. In order to get the license you have to pass a medical and I couldn't do that now since I only have vision in one eye.

We flew the Glasair for about ten years and only had one mishap with it. One day upon landing, the nose gear collapsed due to a faulty part. We just scooted down the runway on our nose and got it stopped. There was no major damage that couldn't be repaired. That is one good thing about a plane of foam and fiberglass; you can easily repair any damage. We were sad though that this happened but thankful that we weren't hurt. Of course our little bird that Glen had named "Sweet P" was down for a month while we repaired it.

Since building airplanes was in our blood, we were getting anxious to build again. The Glasair cost us quite a bit of money to build and we didn't think we could afford to donate it to an organization, so we sold it. Unfortunately, the fellow who bought it got reckless, was showing off by trying to do some aerobatics, and crashed the airplane. It was a fatality. The Federal Aviation Administration (FAA) investigated and reported that the accident was caused by pilot error only, and nothing was wrong with the aircraft.

This was a terrible blow to both of us; not that the aircraft was destroyed, but rather that a life was gone. We both vowed that we would never sell another home-built/experimental airplane, and we didn't.

Our third airplane was a PT-2, similar to an antique Cub Airplane. It was high wing, short take off and landing (STOL) and slow; only cruising about 80 to 90 miles per hour. It was constructed of various materials, fiberglass, metal, and fabric. This took us about one and a half years to build.

I remember one time we were flying home from a fly-in breakfast. We were about 50 miles from our airport and could see a thunderstorm ahead of us. We knew we didn't want to get caught in that, but just couldn't make that airplane go any faster. We both were wishing it had peddles like a bicycle. Then we could have helped it along by peddling as fast as we could; however, once again the Lord was with us and got us safely on the ground a few minutes before the thunderstorm reached the area.

I guess we still liked the "fast" airplanes because after two years we donated this aircraft to the Central State University for training purposes.

Our fourth airplane was a Zenith Zodiac 601, HDS, all metal airplane. By now we were getting fairly proficient in building, and this airplane took us only ten months to build. What a beauty it was, and a lot of fun, but unfortunately we were only able to fly it and enjoy it for about a year. Some devastating news prompted us to donate it to the St. Louis Aviation Museum.

PART IV

FINALE

"Put all your trust in the Lord and do not rely on your own understanding. Think of Him in all your ways, and He will smooth your path" (Proverbs 3:5-6).

My husband, Glen, came home from flying one day and when I looked at him, I knew something was wrong. I said, "What happened?"

He said, "I made a terrible landing. My perception was really off. I must need my eyes examined. I'm not flying anymore until I see what is wrong."

We made an appointment with the optometrist and got his glasses changed, but that didn't seem to help. Problems for him continued.

Glen, like most men, was the sole operator of the TV remote control; click, click, click. He always wanted the TV on, even if he was reading and not watching it. Then one evening he said, "I don't know how to turn on the TV."

I thought he was kidding since I had been teasing him about his buddy, the remote control. However, he made no attempt to turn on the TV, so I came by smiling at him and turned it on. Later at dinner I noticed he was having a hard time figuring out what eating utensil to use, and he started holding his right hand in an odd position. When he got up from the table he was also starting to drag his right foot. My first thought was, he had experienced a stroke and needed to get to a doctor right away. He didn't want to go to the emergency room, so the next morning I called our family doctor and we were able to get an appointment for that afternoon.

After several tests and a MRI it was discovered he had a brain tumor, and he was recommended to an excellent neurosurgeon, who immediately placed him in the hospital. By the next day he was in surgery. The tumor was removed and the doctor felt certain he had gotten it all. However, when the lab results came back a few hours later, it was found to be cancerous, and to quote the doctor, "One of the meanest types of brain cancer!"

Glen continued to get worse. He had two operations, thirty days of radiation and two months of chemotherapy; nothing helped. The doctor seemed to take his case personally. He said, "No matter what I do or try, it doesn't work. It is like God is calling him home." Indeed, He was. We both had to prepare for Glen's death.

We talked, we prayed, we cried, and we grieved together. We shared every thought and feeling as we had always done in the 35 years of our married life. We then decided to go to the local funeral home, where we both prearranged our funerals.

To go to a funeral director and plan your own funeral certainly gives you a strange feeling. In fact, I felt nervous and sad at the same time. However, once it was accomplished, I seemed to feel like a burden had been lifted from my shoulders, and Glen seemed to sense this relief also. Once again we made our decision together, and it would be our final one.

The last three weeks of Glen's life were very hard. He quickly went from walking with a cane to a walker to a wheelchair. Glen was in a lot of pain, and I cared for him in all aspects: feeding, bathing, lifting, etc. He was a large man of six feet, weighing 200 plus pounds. I was short and a little chubby, but far from being a heavyweight. As I look back, I wonder how was I able to lift him and care for him the way I did. My help and my strength had to have come from God.

One night he was in terrible pain. I got him settled into bed and near midnight he had to get up. The pain was nearly unbearable. By this time he couldn't help me all. His strength was gone. I knew I was hurting him just with a touch of my hand. When I tried to get him up and into the wheelchair, his body slipped, with most of it just hanging between the bed and the chair. He cried out in pain. I got down on the floor and somehow was able to get my back under his body and lifted him back onto the bed. I was exhausted and laid beside him to rest a bit. Once I was able to relax and catch my breath, I got up and moved the wheelchair as close as possible to the bed. Somehow I was able to lift him and get him into the wheelchair,

Glen said, "I've got to go to the hospital," so I called 911.

By the time the ambulance got there, I had gotten a bit of strength back and we went for that long ride to the hospital with the sirens screaming. I know now it was only by the grace of God that I was able to lift Glen when he was slipping from the bed.

He was in the hospital for two weeks, requiring an increase of morphine daily. By the end of the two weeks Glen could no longer talk, eat or drink water. He breathed heavily and perspired constantly. I was with him every day and would wipe his face and sponge his mouth every few minutes. I don't know if he was aware of all the visitors who came, but he was always aware of my presence.

Although very weak, he would often reach for my hand and squeeze it. He also appeared to know when our pastor would visit and when prayer was given. Again Glen would squeeze my hand and after prayer he would be more at peace.

He was a good Christian man, attending church every Sunday; even up to the end when he could hardly stand or walk, he would go to church. Glen would often sing at the top of his voice when he was at home and thought no one could hear him. He had a pretty good voice too, but at church he would never sing. However, he would always open the hymnal and seemed to digest every word of the songs being sung. I think he was probably a bit too shy about singing when he thought someone could hear him. Even so, I know Glen loved the Lord, and had put his trust in Him.

It was about 4:30 in the afternoon of November 14. Glen's breathing was so labored and he was wet with perspiration. I was wiping his face with a cool cloth when his breathing stopped and I saw something. It appeared to be a small cloud of white smoke or mist, that came from his mouth or nostrils, and floated over to the window. I stopped wiping his face and thought, *What is that?* It hovered at the window for what seemed to be five to ten seconds, and then it was gone.

Was it his spirit? Was it an angel? Was it his breath of life? After that his breathing started again, but only for a few hours, and he was pronounced dead, November 15. The love of my life was gone, at the age of 63.

I have since read that the body can continue to function to some extent, for a period of time, after actual death has occurred. In my heart I am certain I witnessed my beloved's spirit leaving his body. His rainbow of life had run out, and Glen's final air flight was to join our Heavenly Father.

Taken from The New English Bible, Apocrypha, Wisdom of Solomon, 4:7-15

"But the good man, even if he dies an untimely death, will be at rest. For it is not length of life and number of years which bring the honor due to age; if men have understanding, they have grey hairs enough, and an unspotted life is the true ripeness of age. There was once such a man who pleased God, and God accepted him and took him while still living among sinful men. He was snatched away before his mind could be perverted by wickedness or his soul deceived by falsehood (because evil is like witchcraft; it dims the radiance of good, and the waywardness of desire unsettles an innocent mind); in a short time he came to the perfection of a full span of years. His soul was pleasing to the Lord, who removed him early from a wicked world. The mass of men see this and give it no thought; they do not lay to heart this truth, that those whom God has chosen enjoy his grace and mercy, and that He comes to the help of his holy people."

COME FLY WITH ME

Come fly with me, my love,
To where the sea meets the sky.
We'll watch the rippling water
And the birds wing on high.

Come fly with me, my love,
To where the clouds caress the mountain.
We'll see its snow peaks glisten
Like cotton candy that's just been spun.
Come fly with me, my love,
To where the moon and stars shine bright.
We'll watch the night shadows dancing,
Until the sun warms us with light.

Come fly with me, my love,
We'll be lovers and we'll be friends,
To share these times together,
Until life's rainbow ends.

Written for my beloved husband, on our 25th wedding anniversary. His
life's rainbow ended 10 years later.

ANGELS
STORY NUMBER ONE

Do you believe in angels? If you have read the Bible, perhaps you have noticed that angels are mentioned in nearly every book, from Genesis through Revelations. You may have even had an experience with an angel. Perhaps you didn't see one, but at some time and at some place you may have been guided or sheltered or shielded from danger. When thinking about it, we probably can all tell a story where an angel was a part of our life.

In my job, I was often required to take trips. I usually tried to get a flight early in the day, whereby I'd arrive at my destination before dark. On one particular trip to Alabama, my flight was delayed due to weather. Consequently, I arrived there in the dark, as well as fog and drizzling rain.

I picked up my rental car, looked at the map and headed for my motel. I hadn't gone very far when visibility became nearly zero. I felt myself getting disoriented and scared. I drove and drove for what seemed like hours. Finally I prayed, "God help me. I've got to find a place to stop so I can figure out where I am. Please let me find someone to ask!"

The night had gotten even darker, and there were no other vehicles on the road, nor could I see any road signs to let me know if I was even on the right road. I was so upset I started to cry. Suddenly I saw a turn off to the right. I did not see any signs to tell me where I might be headed, but I knew I had to turn there. The rain was getting heavier and there was still very dense fog. I drove about a quarter of a mile, going down what seemed like a very steep hill and around some curves. Finally I saw some lights! I kept driving towards them and right in front of me was my motel!! Even though I didn't see an angel, surely one guided me safely to my destination.

ANGELS
STORY NUMBER TWO

There was another occasion when my husband and I were traveling south on Interstate Highway 55. We were going to southeast Missouri to visit his mother. We were driving a Volkswagen Rabbit and had our little white poodle with us. All of a sudden the car quit running. Fortunately we were able to get off of the highway. My husband checked under the hood and discovered the timing belt had broken. There was nothing left to do but start walking. (This was before there were cell phones or OnStar systems).

It was an extremely hot day and we walked for probably a mile. Here we were, two adults, dressed nicely, and leading a little white poodle, who had just been groomed the day before.

Cars and trucks zoomed by us. We thought surely someone could see our car was broken down and we needed help, but no one would stop. Finally a car pulled off the road in front of us and came to a stop. It was an old, faded red Pontiac, with several dents and a lot of rust. A black man was driving and all alone. He said, "You want to ride?"

You bet we did! We were so hot and tired, we welcomed any kind of transportation offered to us. My husband sat in the front and the little dog and I got into the back. The inside of the car was not very clean, and there were four onions and a can of pork and beans in a bag on the floor. The fellow didn't give his name, but said he was going fishing. I guessed the onions and beans were going to be his lunch along with any fish he might catch.

A few miles up the road there was a house. We pulled off the main highway and drove up to it. My husband got out of the car and went to the

65

door, while the black man, the dog and myself waited. A white man came to the door and my husband told him, "Our car broke down about ten miles back. Could you call a tow truck for me? I'll be glad to pay you whatever it is worth."

The man looked at the car, looked back at my husband and emphatically responded with, "No, and you all get on out of here!"

My husband turned around and got back in the car and said to the black man, "I'm sorry, but if you are going up the road a little farther, could we ride along?"

The man said, "No need to worry. I saw a station with a tow truck back a ways. I'll take you back there." With that he backtracked nearly 25 miles and stopped at the station he mentioned. We got out and my husband pulled out his wallet to pay him. The man said, "There is no need for money. Just a thank you is enough."

We thanked him several times, shook his hand and walked up to the service station door. We turned to wave goodbye, and he was already gone. He was nowhere to be seen. To this day I believe he was an angel whose purpose was to help us and to possibly test the man at whose home we stopped.

ANGELS
STORY NUMBER THREE

A pastor told this story. Several years ago he drove a school bus for extra money. One evening he was driving some students to a regional basketball game. It had been raining all day and the sides of the road were extremely muddy. Suddenly one of the tires blew out. He was able to get the bus off to the side of the road, but it sank into the mud. No way was he going to be able to drive out of that mud, even if he could have changed the tire. He needed a tow truck.

He didn't know the area, and had no idea who had a tow truck nearby. There were no houses in sight. It was definitely an isolated area. All he could do was pray, "God, what should I do? Help me to get these kids to their ballgame." About that time a huge tow truck came, hooked onto the bus and towed them to a service station.

It would normally be unlikely that a service station would have a tire large enough for a bus; however, they did, and soon the bus was ready to go. The bus driver then asked the tow truck driver, "How much do we owe you?"

The driver replied, "Nothing. God appears dressed in different ways."

I BELIEVE THERE ARE ANGELS AMONG US... DON'T YOU?? POSTSCRIPT

When we are born, our rainbow of life starts. There are good times, bad times, good experiences and bad. Then there comes the end.

Death continues to be a mystery, something the majority of people fear. As Christians, we all know that everything must die, and upon death our suffering here on Earth is over; however, we continue to wonder and most of us feel a bit frightened about the unknown.

My mother-in-law clinically died and she said, "It was the most beautiful thing I have ever seen!" Yet, for some reason no one in her family could bring themselves to ask her just what she saw, and she offered no other information. Perhaps we were to know only that "it was beautiful." However, we all realized she no longer feared but welcomed death.

2 Corinthians 12:2-4

"I know a Christian man who fourteen years ago (whether in the body or out of it, I do not know—God knows) was caught up as far as the third heaven. And I know that this same man (whether in the body or out of it, I do not know—God knows) was caught up into paradise, and heard words so secret that human lips may not repeat them."

My father told of being at the bedside of his mother when she died. She was talking to him when she suddenly said, "I must go now. I hear the angels singing." Those were her last words. She too seemed happy when death came.

Revelation 5:11
"Then as I looked I heard the voices of countless angels...."

I feel God allowed me to see the spirit of my husband leaving his body, and I knew he was no longer in pain. This has been a blessing and a comfort for me. It's something I will never forget, and something that has given me peace.

Our lives are similar to a rainbow. Before we can reach its completeness, we have to experience some rain or bad times. However, with our love and faith in God, we can develop that rainbow into a beautiful life, and find the pot of gold in God's Heavenly home.

"In his heart a man plans his course, but the Lord determines his steps" (Proverbs:16:9).